Joel and the Great Merlini

JOEL and the GREAT MERLINI

by Eloise Jarvis McGraw
Illustrated by Jim Arnosky

PANTHEON BOOKS

For Adam
From Granny

Library of Congress Cataloging in Publication Data
McGraw, Eloise Jarvis. Joel and the great Merlini.
Summary: With a great deal of practice and help from an already accomplished magician, Joel perfects his magic act. Afterwards he wonders if it is too perfect.
[1. Magic—Fiction] I. James E. Arnosky. II. Title.
PZ7.M1696Jo 1979 [Fic] 79-4580
ISBN 0-394-94193-X   ISBN 0-394-94193-4 lib. bdg.

Joel and the Great Merlini

·1·

When Joel Penny first discovered magic (at about age four) he thought it would be easy. He thought all you had to do was *concentrate,* then bunch all five fingers into a point, jab it at something, and say *Ka-zaaam!* and the thing would just disappear. Or turn into something else. Or whatever.

That idea lasted about as long as the tenth *Ka-zaaam*.

By the time he was six or seven, he was convinced it was all a matter of the right *equipment*. If he could just send for all the stuff in the catalogs—black boxes with trick bottoms, top hats with trick tops, tiny cardboard tubes packed with different colored flags that you could hide in your sleeve, and dozens of other things—he'd have it made. He'd soon be astounding everybody with an act as good as the one Weirdo the Wizard put on for Lions' Club Carnivals and the Church Ladies' Fair.

He did collect a lot of equipment. One birthday

his mother gave him Bixby's Mixed Tricks, and for Christmas he got Professor Mo's Magic Set. The next Christmas his granny topped those with the Mammoth Master Magician's Box Including Hat and Wand. He learned to do most of the tricks, too—mainly by practicing on his family.

For a couple of years there he was always cornering his mother or his father or his granny or his little brother Sammy, and saying "Think of a number between one and sixty-three," then making them point to whichever one of six special lists they saw it on. Then, after a long, glassy-eyed moment of staring at the lists, he'd burst out with their number. After a while he got so he could burst out with it in just a second, with no staring.

That trick improved his arithmetic no end.

And there were lots of others. He could tuck a dollar bill into the *left* side of Bixby's Magic Wallet, close the wallet, then open it to show the dollar on the *right*. Or simply gone. He could riffle through Professor Mo's Miracle Playing Cards to show an (apparently) ordinary deck, then riffle through again to show all Aces of Spades. He'd even invented a way to pull a homemade paper rabbit right out of the

Mammoth Box top hat. By the time he was nine he had an act good enough so that little kids, at least, were astounded, and grownups pretended to be. He presented it at Parents' Night, at school, and made a hit.

But *then* he discovered a book in the library about famous magicians—Houdini, and Blackstone, and a lot of others. It opened a whole world Joel hadn't known was there—the world of locks and bolts and knotted ropes and miraculous escapes, and the sort of magic called sleight of hand. He bought himself a book of coin and card tricks and a pair of handcuffs, which he began to work with feverishly. Before Thanksgiving he had discovered, all by himself, a secret way to open the handcuffs while they were on his wrists, and bring off a real escape, just like Houdini's. From then on it was his favorite trick— and a different *kind* of trick from any he'd ever done before. It sort of spoiled the old kind for him. Real magic, he was just now realizing at age ten or so, wasn't just gadgets anybody could buy in a store. Real magic was something you did *yourself*. It was the skill of your own fingers and brain, and you got it in one way only—by practice, practice, practice. That's what all the great ones said—Houdini and Blackstone and the rest.

Well, better late than never. I'm fairly young yet, Joel told himself.

So he practiced. He nearly wore out quarters and half-dollars and decks of cards and got himself accused of living in a dream world because half the time he was concentrating so hard on sleight of hand that he didn't know what was going on around him. His schoolwork suffered. His baseball suffered (it was getting to be spring by now). And Joel suffered, because even after all that practicing, his fingers felt about as skillful as a bunch of sausages. Sausages with little lead weights tied on the ends.

His little brother, Sammy, couldn't understand why he bothered with something you had to try over and over and over. "How come you don't do those good tricks with your magic wallet anymore?" Sammy asked one day.

"Because they're only gimmick tricks," Joel explained. "I want to do real ones. Like making this fifty-cent piece disappear. I can *almost* do it." He tried again, and then again (dropping the coin both times) and then once more, this time managing to ease the coin around to the back of his hand and out of sight—but so slowly there was no mystery to it at all. "These are great tricks when they're done right," Joel said doggedly. "Want me to show you how to do one?"

"No, I like that magic wallet better," Sammy said.

"Well, you can have it," said Joel, and gave him the whole Bixby's Mixed Tricks set.

Sammy gave a yell of delight, grabbed the set, and ran up to his own room. Half an hour later, Joel's granny, who lived with them, put her head in his doorway. "Did you give Sammy that magic set for keeps?" she asked. When Joel said he had, she came right in and hugged him. "That was mighty nice and generous of you, Joel Penny! Just for that you ought to get anything you wish for!"

Joel was a little startled, because he didn't remember feeling especially generous or nice, but he didn't want to spoil Granny's pleasure, so he kept quiet.

·2·

The next afternoon—it was Wednesday the 13th of April, as he remembered all his life—his teacher, Miss Honeywell, stopped him as he was leaving school. "Joel, about the Stunt Nite next week. You're doing your magic act, aren't you?" she asked in a voice that meant she wanted "yes" for an answer, and no hedging.

"Well," Joel hedged.

"Now Joel—I need you on that program!"

"But I already gave that act for Parents' Night last fall. And again at Christmas. The very same act!"

"Just change it around a little," said Miss Honeywell. "Add something new."

"But I haven't really—"

"Joel, don't argue. You've got ten whole days to get ready. Now I'm *counting* on you."

Joel gave up, said "Yes, Miss Honeywell," and went on home, feeling as if he were wearing cement boots and a backpack full of bricks. The heaviest part was remembering how glad and eager he would have felt, just a few months ago, to put on a magic act for anybody, anywhere, at a moment's notice, with his gadgets and things. He almost wished he had never heard of Houdini or read any books at all.

Ten whole days to get ready. "Ha, *ha!*" Joel said bitterly, and Tagalong, his sort-of terrier, who had run down the porch steps to meet him, stopped guiltily and flattened her ears. "It's okay, I didn't mean you," Joel told her, giving the ears a quick rub in passing. He trudged on upstairs to his room.

Just add something new. Ha, *ha.* The only new thing he'd learned since Christmas was two beginner's coin tricks, and one of them wasn't smooth yet.

He sighed, opened his desk drawer and got out the stuff for the coin trick that wasn't smooth yet, and started to practice. It was a dandy trick, part gimmick, but mostly sleight of hand. What you *appeared* to do was make four coins pass right through the bottom of a little paper cup, through a handkerchief, and into a second paper cup (without, of course, damaging the handkerchief in any way) and after that, make the coins fly invisibly from one cup to the other, holding the cups far apart.

What you *really* were doing was a lot of tricky juggling with *three* little cups, slipping the two public ones into or off of the secret third one, which you kept hidden in your hand by means of a little tab pinched between two fingers. Or tried to keep hidden. It was all a great deal harder than it seemed.

He worked at it about ten minutes, then dropped the cups back into his drawer and plodded dismally down to the kitchen. His mother was still at her job, but his granny was there, having a cup of coffee and a dill pickle, which was her favorite after-school snack. Of course she didn't go to school, but she usually had something with Sammy when he came home at two-thirty, then something with Joel when he got there at four.

"Thought you'd stood me up," said his granny, putting a powdered sugar doughnut on a plate for him.

"Oh, I wouldn't do that," Joel told her, managing a sort of smile in spite of the way he was feeling. "I was just—busy in my room." He took an enormous bite of the doughnut so he'd be unable to answer questions in case she wanted to discuss it. Being Granny (he should have remembered) she didn't ask any, just took another sip of coffee. So immediately *he* wanted to discuss it. He could hardly wait until his mouth was empty. "Granny," he said with a little puff of powdered sugar. "Listen, you remember when you were learning to ski that time you told us about, when Mommie and Uncle Oliver were kids, and you kept falling down and couldn't get back up?"

"Oh, I remember," Granny assured him.

"Well . . . how did you finally get so you could do it?"

"Just kept trying."

"Oh," said Joel. Practice, practice, practice, she meant. He took another bite of doughnut and sighed, raising a whole little cloud of powdered sugar. "I *have* kept trying," he said. "What if a person's just naturally clumsy at—whatever it is?"

Granny took another dill pickle and thought about that. "I don't think it matters," she said. "Babies are naturally clumsy at walking, to begin with, but they all learn. Some faster than others. Took me three or

four years to learn to ski. Talk about naturally clumsy!"

"Three or four *years*?" Joel echoed, feeling as if a lot more bricks had been added to his backpack. He put his elbow on the table beside the doughnut plate and heaved another sigh. Powdered sugar flew everywhere, in a sort of smoke screen.

"I can see I should have got chocolate ones today," observed his granny. "Well, you could try wishing, along with practicing. On stars and wishbones and so on. I did a lot of hard wishing, let me tell you, all those days I kept falling down in the snow."

Joel raised his chin from his hand. "Honest? You think it helped?"

"I don't know about *helped,* but I never thought it did any harm," said Granny.

·3·

That evening, coming home with Tagalong from an after-dinner walk around the block, Joel just happened to see the evening star appearing above the roof next door. He also just happened to see it over his left shoulder. There was no sense passing up a chance like that. He stood still and muttered rapidly, *"Star light, star bright, first starasee tonight, I wishamay I wishamight, have the wishawish tonight.* And I *wish* I could do *real magic."*

Before he had time to feel stupid, or even to warn himself not to expect anything, there was a puff of smoke—pink smoke, like a cloud at sunset—and out of it stepped a tall, skinny man in a funny fog-gray nightshirt. Tagalong gave one terrified bark and ran for home. Joel was too startled to do anything but stare. The man had very little hair on his head but a lot on his face, divided into bushy white eyebrows and a long, flowing beard like Father Time's. His nightshirt was something like Father Time's, too, except it was embroidered all over with silver moons and stars and numbers and things. In one hand he held a top hat, in the other a wand with a silver tip.

"Ah! There you are, Joel my boy!" he exclaimed. "It *is* Joel, isn't it?"

"Y-yessir," stammered Joel.

"Well! Delighted, I'm sure! I am Merlini the Great."

"Yessir," said Joel again. Then, as he realized what he was hearing, he gasped, "Wow. Are you a magician?"

"The very best! Merlini the *Great,* you know. It's embroidered somewhere on my robe. Here it is! No —that's something else. Here! No, that's my recipe for taffy. Perhaps it's around in back some place." Merlini was twisting and turning his long body, peering down at his ankles and back over his shoulder. "Oh, well," he said with a wide, cheerful smile that quirked up at the corners like a waxed moustache. "You'll take my word for it, won't you?"

"Yessir," Joel said faintly. "Please sir, do you mean —did you come because I made that wish?"

"Of course. That's my . . ." Merlini paused to search for a word, then pounced on it with triumph, "my *avocation.* Coming when someone wishes. 'Avocation' comes from a Latin word meaning 'called away,' you understand," he added brilliantly.

Joel wasn't sure he did. "You mean everytime anybody makes a wish, anywhere in the world—"

"Oh, I don't answer *every* wish. Oh, no, no, dear boy, I'd be run off my legs. Getting too old for that sort of nonsense now. No, I pick and choose."

"Among the wishes? How do you decide?" Joel marveled.

"I choose the one that pulls hardest," Merlini told him. "Yours pulled like sixty, Joel my boy. *I wish I could learn real magic.* Heard you plain as day. Now tell me, what would you like to learn first?"

"I don't know," Joel said. He pinched himself to see if he was dreaming. He was not. Merlini was right there, plainly visible in the pale blue evening light, looking at him expectantly. Quick, ask him something! Joel urged himself. "Well, I've been working on a flying-coins trick," he burst out. "And on making a fifty-cent piece disappear."

"Ah! Disappearances. Very wise to start with basics. Let me see. I don't have a fifty-cent piece, but would you care to make that fireplug disappear? Here, just borrow my wand. Now touch the fireplug and tell it to vanish."

"Fireplug?" Joel echoed, feeling he somehow lost his place in the conversation. However, he took the wand—it felt strange and heavy in his hand— touched the fireplug, and said, "Vanish."

It vanished. Instantly. Completely. There wasn't even a hole in the sidewalk. With a gasp Joel sat

down abruptly on the curb, staring from the un-broken cement to the wand in his hand.

"There! Now wasn't that easy?" Merlini was saying in a pleased voice. "Very nicely done, too."

"But—please, sir, would you explain the trick? I mean—where did it go?" Joel entreated.

"Go?" Merlini seemed puzzled. "Why, my boy, I don't know that I can answer that. It never occurred to me to wonder where things go when they vanish."

"You mean it's really *gone*? It's not just a—an illusion? This is really *real* magic?"

"Of course! That's what you wanted, wasn't it?" As Joel failed to answer, Merlini added with a touch of severity, "It's what you *said*."

"I only meant real *tricks*," Joel said in a voice he could hardly hear himself. But his eyes stretched wider and wider as possibilities undreamed-of since the old *Ka-zaaam* days began to open in his mind. "Wow!" he whispered. "WOW!"

·4·

Merlini beamed down at him and rubbed his hands together. "Now then, what shall we do next?"

Joel leaped to his feet, then hesitated. "Don't you think we'd better put the fireplug back?" he asked a bit anxiously. "Because what if there was a fire?"

"An excellent thought, my boy. Level-headed! You shall do it yourself. Just wave the wand—watch my hand a moment—like this, see? Then command the fireplug to reappear in its place. Be sure to say, 'in its place.'"

Joel obeyed. There was a very small puff of the pink smoke, and the fireplug was right where it had been before. Joel's grin spread across his face until he felt as if it touched his ears. Quickly he dug in his pocket and found his coin. "Could you teach me how to make this disappear?" he asked. "I've been working and working on it, but every time I get it halfway around my hand, like this, I—oh!" Joel blinked at his empty hand, looked around on the ground and then at Merlini, who smiled his waxed-moustache smile and said slyly, "Look in your left pants pocket."

Joel thrust in his hand. The coin was there. Merlini burst out laughing, and Joel laughed a little too, though he felt rather confused about who the trick was on. "I only meant—teach me how to make it *look* like it disappears," he explained. "You know, just teach me to do the *trick*."

"But my dear boy! What you just did was worth a hundred tricks!" Merlini exclaimed, clapping him on the back.

There was really no question about that. Why am I bothering about *my* kind of magic, anyhow? Joel thought. Merlini's is so much better! "What shall I try next, then?" he asked Merlini.

"Anything you like, dear boy! Let your imagination soar! That's what I do."

Joel tried, but *his* imagination kept bumbling and bumping into things like a fly in a bottle. Flights of fancy had never been his strong point. "Could I turn that pebble into a cupcake?" he offered rather awkwardly.

"Just touch it with the wand."

Joel did so, and found himself holding a pink-frosted cupcake. Dizzily he touched it again, and it turned back into a pebble.

"That's the ticket!" Merlini exclaimed with a hearty backslap that sent the pebble spinning from Joel's hands. "Try something harder!"

Joel tried making the next-door-neighbor's mailbox turn upside down and stand on its little flag. No problem. Then he made it vanish. It did so. Drunk with power, he commanded it to reappear. It reappeared on a tree branch six feet above his head.

"You forgot to say 'in its place,'" explained Merlini.

Slightly shaken, Joel corrected his mistake, and was relieved when he'd settled the mailbox firmly on its post. Privately he decided to leave the neighbors' property alone.

"Oh, that's topnotch, my boy," Merlini was saying. "Just tip-top! You have quite a touch, you know, really you do. Tell me, isn't there some school program coming up soon?" he added eagerly. "We could get a little act prepared."

"Well, there's Stunt Nite. That's why I—but it's ten whole days away."

"Why, that's splendid! Just the thing!"

"You mean you'll still be here ten days from now?" Joel cried.

"Oh, I think I can spare the time. I *will* spare it, anyhow. You're much more fun than most wish-makers."

"And you'll help me with my act?"

"I'd like nothing better!" Merlini beamed at him, then added, "Mind you, we'll have to work like sixty, every day."

"Oh, I will! I'll work like seventy!" Joel promised joyfully. Then, as the porch light at his house went on, and his mother stuck her head out, calling, "Joel?

Where are you?" he caught Merlini's embroidered sleeve and tugged him into the shadows. "The trouble is," he whispered, "they keep me awful busy. There's school, and homework, and yard work, and . . . Where will I find you? When can we—"

"Don't worry about a thing, my boy," Merlini whispered back. "When you're free, you'll find my wand in your pocket."

Joel glanced down at the wand he was holding, and found he was no longer holding it. He glanced up, and Merlini was no longer beside him. "Wow," he said softly. "Oh, *wow*. Oh *boy!*" Taking a deep, excited breath that felt as if it might burst off all his shirt buttons, ping, ping, ping, ping, he bounded up the street toward the lighted front porch.

·5·

The next ten days were the most exciting Joel had ever spent. Finding time to practice was no problem. Merlini found bits of spare time lying about everywhere, simply cluttering up the day. Walking to school in the morning, Joel would suddenly discover the wand in his pocket and Merlini beside him. At bedtime, he would no sooner turn out his light than Merlini was bending over his bed, whispering that they could practice disappearances by moonlight. There were ten-minute patches between dinner and homework, and a full hour or so after school, because Joel's share of the yard work became nothing at all when he could just touch a weed with Merlini's wand and make it vanish. Even during lunch hour at school, if Joel ever found himself alone, Merlini was sure to turn up.

In fact, he scarcely ever found himself alone, even long enough to practice his old tricks from the coin-and-card-trick book, which he kept plugging away at, although he hardly knew why. "I'd still like to learn a few," he told Merlini apologetically one evening in his room. "Just to see if I can, I guess."

"Why, you shall learn a dozen if you like, my boy! We'll try them *immedjitly*! My memory's not what it was," Merlini added as he began to pull his long robe this way and that, craning his neck to read upside down. "But I'm sure I have notes on several embroidered here somewhere . . ."

"I've got a book we can use," Joel said hastily. "If I could just palm a coin better, I could do all sorts of good tricks. And then there's a trick with little paper cups—here, I'll show you. You're supposed to make it look like the coins are going right through the handkerchief, or flying from one cup to the other—but you've really got *three* cups, see, and I always drop the secret one when I . . ."

But this time the trick came out perfectly. With a gasp of pleasure, Joel poured the coins out of the right-hand cup, and turned the left-hand one upside down, with the secret third one as securely concealed in his palm as if it were glued there.

"Why, I did it!" he yelled joyfully. Then he threw a sudden glance at Merlini, who was looking like the cat that swallowed the goldfish. "Or did *you* help?" he added.

"I only helped a *little*," Merlini said quickly. "Helped you learn it. And didn't it come out tip-top?"

"Oh, yes, it did! But—will it come out tip-top next time, when you're not around to coach me?" Joel persisted.

"Oh, I'm going to be around a while, don't you

worry about that! Why, I'm having the time of my life! Now suppose we add a little effect to that trick with the cups, eh? We might pour out gumdrops instead of coins, how would that be? Or possibly a flock of tiny canaries, all singing . . ."

It was just no use trying to get Merlini down to the humdrum level of ordinary regular magic. And why should I when he's teaching me *his* kind? Joel asked himself, feeling a rush of affection for his strange friend, who was twisting his long body into bow-knots trying to locate something on his robe— possibly the recipe for gumdrops. The thing to do was learn all the *real* magic possible before Saturday, because once Stunt Nite was over, Merlini would undoubtedly go back to wherever he came from. Joel didn't even want to think about that.

·6·

By Saturday, Joel's act was worked out in detail—not only the program of tricks, which was Merlini's department, but the talking and razzle-dazzle, which was Joel's. "Because a person's got to have a good line of patter, to go with the tricks," Joel had explained to Merlini, who seemed quite inexperienced in ordinary stage work. "All the books say so. They call it 'misdirection'—you know, making the audience watch your left hand while you do something secret with your right hand. Like if I was pretending to change this nickel to a quarter."

"But you won't be pretending," Merlini reminded him with a wink. "You're really going to do it."

"Well . . . I know." Joel gazed just a bit uneasily at the nickel in his hand, which changed obediently to a quarter and back again. "To tell the truth, Merlini," he confessed, "I don't think I want that to get around."

"I understand, dear boy. You think problems might arise," Merlini said tactfully.

Relieved, Joel nodded. He had been visualizing, in awful detail, the problems that would certainly arise if his brother Sammy—or anybody—found out he could really change nickels into quarters. "There's another thing," he added. "While I'm onstage— where are you going to be?"

"Close enough to prompt you if you forget,"

Merlini assured him. "But I'll stay well hidden! Nobody will dream you're not alone."

So that evening at 9:15 (he was last on the program) Joel walked onstage all alone, carrying a little table and Merlini's wand, and began at once to make school history. He changed a nickle to a quarter, then the quarter to a half-dollar, then the half-dollar to a piggybank full of dimes. He changed a rock to a skateboard, and rode around the stage. He reached into thin air and produced a bunch of flowers, then made the flowers explode like firecrackers at a touch. When the smoke cleared he removed from his head a top hat nobody had seen there before. From the hat he drew a rabbit, which changed to a Saint Bernard while the audience was looking at the Swiss flag Joel had discovered in the footlights. At Joel's command, the Saint Bernard took the flag in his mouth and jumped neatly back into the hat, which as neatly vanished in another puff of smoke.

By now, the audience was cheering wildly, Joel's teacher was gaping at him as if she had never seen him before, and his parents and brother were sitting frozen with astonishment. Only his granny seemed unsurprised—but then she had never underestimated

Joel's abilities, or the Mammoth Magic Box she had given him, either.

Joel had not finished. While the cheers still rang, he pulled a whole line of wash from his pants pocket —shirts and pillow cases and sheets and socks—until it stretched clear across the stage. Then he snapped his fingers in the air, and all the white sheets changed to pink, after which he reeled the whole line back into a little wad, put the wad in his pocket, and bowed. He walked offstage to thunderous applause, over which piercing whistles curved like Fourth-of-July rockets.

An encore was obviously demanded. His heart beginning to pound with excitement, Joel walked back onstage to the little table and opened its drawer, in which—without bothering to mention it to Merlini— he had privately stowed the two tiny paper cups and the secret third one, for his flying-coins trick. Counting four quarters into the first cup, he opened a handkerchief with a dramatic snap, draped it over his hand, and set the cup on top of it. He picked up the other cup—tipping it to show how empty it was—and put it *under* the handkerchief. Then with a flourish and a casual flick of his thumb and finger, he sent the full cup rolling on the table, now perfectly empty.

It remained only to reach under the handkerchief and produce cup number two, out of which the quarters now spilled. He did the whole thing perfectly.

The applause was mild. The audience seemed to be waiting for more.

Well, there was more to the trick. Hastily scooping up the coins, Joel counted them back into cup number one, held in his right hand. He then picked up cup number two in his left. Holding them as far apart as he could reach, he commanded the coins to fly from one cup to the other. And he did that perfectly too. The coins were safe in the secret third cup clamped between his left fingers, which he'd neither dropped nor exposed when he slipped cup number two deftly over it. Flushing red to his ears with triumph—it was the smoothest the trick had *ever* gone—Joel proudly upended "empty" cup number two to let the coins roll out.

Instead, out poured a flock of tiny bright canaries, all singing their heads off. They swirled upward, circled once around Joel's top hat, then swooped out over the audience and began to dart about like shooting stars.

Joel's protesting "Hey!" was lost in the din of

shrieks and laughter. He stared at the wild flutter of birds, then into his empty paper cup—then, abruptly, into the wings offstage. He was in time to see a tell-tale little drift of pink smoke still clinging to the curtain. The canaries, by now, had become mere sparks of light, which winked out as they slowly drifted downward over the whooping, cheering audience.

There was really nothing for Joel to do but bow.

·7·

It could truthfully be said—and Joel's teacher and the principal both said it, several times, in loud astonished voices—that the Elm Hills Elementary School Spring Stunt Nite had never had such a bang-up finale. Everybody else said the same, and more, as they swarmed around Joel in the main hall afterward. He got awfully confused and tired of being bombarded with questions, and even tireder of grinning apologetically and telling everybody, including his family and a lady from the local newspaper who was *very* persistent—that good magicians never reveal their secrets. The minute he got home he did a vanishing act himself, and went upstairs to bed.

He was not really surprised to find Merlini waiting for him in his room, wearing a wide, excited smile. "Well, my boy! Didn't it all go famously? You did a tip-top job, tip-top! We're quite a team, eh?" Joel made suitable noises of agreement and thanks, which Merlini brushed away with a hearty, "Not-a-tall, not-a-tall, my pleasure!" Then he added rather cautiously, "Tell me, dear boy—how did you like my little —mm—contribution to your encore? I didn't think you'd . . . mind . . . ?"

"Oh. No. The canaries, you mean," Joel said. "They were fine. I mean, they were really great."

"Oh dear, you did mind," Merlini said, sitting down on the edge of Joel's bed.

Joel stared at his thumbnail, wishing he could say something really appreciative and mean it. He had been trying hard, ever since he walked offstage, to be grateful to Merlini for those canaries and he just couldn't. He kept feeling the way Granny must feel when Dad told the end of her joke for her. "You stole my thunder!" she always said indignantly, whether she'd forgotten the end herself, or not.

"It's only—you stole my thunder," Joel blurted. "I wanted the encore to be *mine*."

"But it really was yours. I only added a tiny dazzle at the end. I do apologize, dear boy," Merlini said in quite an abject tone. "I see now I shouldn't have interfered. But at the time—well, I could see that flying-coins trick just wasn't *taking*. Oh, it's a splendid trick, you understand, simply splendid—but not . . . following directly after the . . . the ones that went before, d'you see? I . . . the people weren't clapping. I couldn't bear to have you disappointed."

A person just couldn't stay mad at Merlini. He meant so well. Joel could feel himself begin to go all mushy inside. "Oh, that's okay," he mumbled. "Honest." He thrust out his hand and even managed a smile.

"Oh, I *am* glad," Merlini said, shaking hands earnestly. "I do want us to go on being partners. Now I'll leave *at once* so you can go to bed. See you tomorrow!" He smiled, and disappeared with such speed that Joel was left still holding a little handful of pink smoke.

He sighed, opened his hand, and watched the smoke trail away into nothing. Then he realized what

Merlini had said. To go on being partners, and "see you tomorrow" sounded very much as if Merlini intended to go right on being around to teach him, whether Stunt Nite was over or not.

But am I actually learning anything? Joel wondered as he got into his pajamas. Maybe *he's* doing all the magic, really, and I'm just making the motions—like with those canaries.

He stopped in the middle of climbing into bed.

He'd never tried any *real* magic, Merlini's magic, by himself—mainly because he was almost never by himself, and when he was, he was practicing furiously on the old card and coin tricks. But I can do it, he reassured himself. Can't I? It's always seemed so easy.

Now that the question had occurred to him, he had to know the answer. Turning to face his room as if it were an audience, he reached into thin air to grasp the bunch of flowers for the exploding flower trick. No flowers appeared in his hand, exploding or otherwise.

Maybe that's a really hard one, he told himself quickly. I'll just . . .

There was a nickel on his desk. He held it on his palm and commanded it to change to a quarter Nothing whatever happened.

So that was that. After a moment, slowly and reluctantly, Joel began to fish around in the pockets of his jacket, hanging on the chair. There was one more question to answer. Locating the three little paper cups and the four coins, he took a long breath and went through the flying-coins trick, from start to finish. It turned out perfectly—both parts. Just perfectly. Though with no canaries.

He sat down on his bed, thinking hard.

So he hadn't actually learned a bit of magic in the whole ten days. Not *real* magic, Merlini's kind. He'd learned a little of his own kind—by practice, practice, practice—but Merlini's kind worked only when Merlini was around.

For me, it's no better than gimmick magic, Joel thought. Just a bigger and better Professor Mo's set.

Feeling a bit stunned, he switched off the light and got under the covers.

·8·

Before anybody was up the next morning, Joel took a long bike ride, clear out to the edge of town. Leaving his bike at the foot of Parson's Hill, he climbed to the top and sat down on his favorite rock to stare out over the valley and try to work things out. In about three seconds, as he'd more or less expected, Merlini stepped out from behind a tree, wearing his quirked-up, cheerful smile.

"*Good* morning, Joel my boy!" he exclaimed. "You're out bright and early. Lovely morning, isn't it? What shall we work on first? I know a splendid variation on that Saint Bernard trick."

"Merlini," Joel said, coming straight to the point, "we've got to have a talk. About things. If you don't mind."

"Yes," sighed Merlini. "I rather thought you'd say that." He sat down on another rock, eyeing Joel anxiously. "Ah . . . still a bit upset about the canaries?"

"No. Honest. I understand now, and it's okay.

What I want to talk about is from now on." Joel paused. He cleared his throat. This was harder than he'd expected. "I—I'm sort of taking it for granted there's going to *be* a 'from now on?' " he added awkwardly.

"Oh, I do hope so," Merlini said, clasping his hands together so hard his knuckles stood out like little knobs. "I've never had such a splendid time on a wish-call. Not ever. Really. I'm very fond of you, my boy."

"Well—thanks, Merlini. I like you, too. It's just—"

"And a chap gets tired of this dashing about," Merlini went on in a fretful tone. "Now here, now there—at anybody's beck and call. Not as young as I was, y'know. Be lovely to just settle down right here—go partners with you, eh? Charming neighborhood. And such a nice century, too."

"Yes. Well, I thought you might be feeling that way. It's why we've got to have a—sort of agreement."

"Oh, whatever you say, dear boy."

"Well, the thing is, Merlini, last night I got to thinking, and I realized those exploding flowers and all—I didn't make them happen. Any more than I did the canaries. *You* did."

"Ah . . . well, my boy—" began Merlini unhappily.

"But that's okay too," Joel assured him. "I see now I couldn't ever learn that kind of magic anyway. And when I first made that wish, you know, all I wanted was to learn the *regular* kind, like with coins and cards and sleight of hand. So if this *real* kind is something I can never learn anyhow, well . . . I don't think I want to go any further with it. I'd rather you helped me with the sleight of hand."

Joel drew a breath of relief. He'd said it, and got it all straight.

Merlini was combing his fingers through his beard, blinking rather sadly at the view. "Oh, you *can* learn the real sort. I did, once upon a time. And you have quite a knack, you know. But it does take *such* a lot of practice—and why should you bother with all that, dear boy, when I can just stay in the background and help you?"

"You mean *you* had to practice too?" Joel said, staring at him. It was hard to picture Merlini getting things mixed up or dropping them, or reaching into thin air for flowers that refused to appear. "For about how long?" he asked warily.

"Ever so long," confessed Merlini. "About seven hundred years."

They looked at each other in silence a moment. Then Joel said, "I'd rather learn sleight of hand."

"Yes. Well, I thought you might. Very well, it shall be just as you like, my boy. You boss the partnership, and I'll give you all the assistance I can."

"And no canaries," added Joel.

"No." Merlini smiled rather weakly. "I will endeavor to restrain myself." He looked a trifle depressed for a moment, and sighed once or twice, but presently his smile came back, this time with the corners quirked up.

"I'll show you a card sleight—if I can remember it," he offered. Twisting about, he picked up the hem of his robe and studied it in several places, then tossed it aside.

"Yes, I have it now. Let me see, I'll need a full deck."

He plucked a deck of cards out of nowhere, shuf-

fled them briskly on a small table that had suddenly appeared between him and Joel, and spread them with a swift flourish which Joel recognized at once.

"That's the Ribbon Spread!" he exclaimed. "I can almost do that. It's in my book!"

"What? Oh, the flourish. Quite. Now, just pick a card, any card."

"Okay." Joel picked one. "And then will you help me get my Ribbon Spread that smooth?"

·9·

The new agreement held very well for a day or two, with Merlini scrupulously limiting his kind of magic to plucking cards and other props out of the air, and leaving Joel's kind strictly to Joel. Joel not only got his Ribbon Spread smooth, he added two Pyramid variations to it, learned the Charlier Cut—which was very important for future tricks—and the Jog Shuffle, and how to keep a certain card on top without seeming to do so, plus a couple of good coin sleights. He was overjoyed, and Merlini got into the spirit and hunted up all sorts of old beginner's stuff he had embroidered here and there on his robe from his own youth (about six hundred and eighty-nine years ago, as Joel figured it, with awe) and seemed to enjoy proving he could still do it.

For a day or two.

Then the requests for Joel's act began to come in, word having got around about his Stunt Nite performance. He managed to dodge the Lions' Club and the Main Street Merchants, whose meetings conflicted with school, but the next invitation was from the Community Club, of which both his parents were members, and he really couldn't get out of that. Nor could he get by with just his flying-coins trick and a few sleights, either—they wanted the Stunt Nite act, Saint Bernard and all. And the persistent newspaper lady came to the meeting, with a photographer. The next morning, there was Joel on the front page, pulling the laundry line out of his pocket.

After that things got clear out of hand. The phone began to ring and Joel began to get four or five letters a day, all from people wanting him to perform, or be interviewed, or be on TV. Merlini got out of hand too. He got terribly excited by the stir Joel was causing, and far from helping him cool it down, he kept adding new little touches every time Joel did the act, to stir things up even more. There was no use trying to hold him to his promise. Even when they were practicing all alone, Merlini just couldn't resist making Joel's kind of magic tricks a little better than they were. And whenever Joel tried to slip a coin-sleight in as an encore, it wound up topping the show.

By this time every request had become a demand,

and Joel was at his wits' end. One Saturday morning just as he hung up the phone after giving in to another insistent program chairman—the Church Ladies' Fair this time—his granny came along the upstairs hall.

"Trouble, Joel?" she said, stopping beside him.

"I was just thinking—Weirdo the Wizard must not be getting any business at all these days."

"Are they paying you, all these clubs and things?"

"No."

"Then your price is better than his, I'll bet. Your act is a lot better, too," Granny added with a penetrating look at Joel. "If it *weren't* so good, some of them might decide Weirdo wasn't so bad."

"That's true," Joel sighed. "I get your point." It was sound advice, like most of Granny's. He would gladly have made his act the worst in town right away, had it been possible. Unfortunately, it was not possible. Not with Merlini in the background, eager to turn the least bungle—planned or otherwise—into some fresh marvel.

Joel plodded on downstairs and outside to touch a few dandelions with Merlini's wand and make them vanish, almost longing for the days when he'd had to get down on his knees and grub them out. At least then he knew he'd *done* something at the end of a Saturday morning. In fact, he was beginning to long for the time before he ever laid eyes on Merlini—those lovely, uneventful days when he could just plug along on his own, and if he happened to accomplish something, especially a magic trick, he could be sure it really *was* on his own.

Maybe the greatest thing in the world, Joel mused as he went in to wash his hands for lunch, was just to be left alone to do things by yourself.

But for him, it was turning out to be the hardest thing in the world to achieve. It seemed so simple—but how did you make it happen? Practice, practice, practice wasn't the answer to this one. Neither was wishing on stars or wishbones, as he found out by a few private trials and failures over the next few days. Neither was anything else he could think of, and before long he was thinking of nothing else.

And then, quite suddenly one day, he had an idea, unlike any he'd had before. It was breathtakingly simple—so simple he couldn't honestly believe it would work, but so logical he had to try it.

·10·

That afternoon, he walked along past the school to the little patch of woods at the end of the street, where he and Merlini often practiced. As usual, Merlini was waiting for him impatiently, bursting with ideas for the Church Ladies' Fair, which was coming up next week.

"But I was sort of hoping to get out of that," Joel told him. "I mean, I might pretend to be sick or something."

"Nonsense, my boy! You can't leave the good ladies in the lurch, now can you? Who could they get to replace you? And what would your mother say? Isn't she a member?"

"They could get Weirdo. And my mother *might* help me get out of it. She didn't like my arithmetic grade last week one bit."

"Oh, my. I don't wish to interfere with your studies, dear boy, not for a minute," Merlini said anxiously. "Perhaps I could help you with your arithmetic. I used to be quite good at—" Merlini was already scanning the hem of his nightshirt.

"No! I mean, no thanks, Merlini—all I need is to cut down on these programs." Maybe, Joel thought, he'd understand if I could just *explain*. "The act's too *good,* you see, for a kid my age. These clubs and things wouldn't want me if I could only do kid stuff, maybe a few coin and card sleights."

"Oh, quite right, my boy—nothing much to those. Not that we won't keep practicing sleights," Merlini added quickly. "I know you're fond of them. But just at the moment I want to tell you a few ideas I've had. Here, suppose you limber up with a few little transformations, while I talk."

Joel gave up. With a sigh, he took the wand Merlini was holding out to him, and did as he was told, while Merlini sat on a stump and described all the dazzlements he had planned for the Church Ladies. They were many and marvelous, and Joel did not really bother to listen.

"And then how would it be," Merlini was saying, "if we changed a whole lot of drinking straws into little souvenir magician's wands, so the ladies could sell them at their bazaar? I think they'd appreciate that. Or we might ask one lady for a hairpin, and stretch the hairpin into a croquet wicket, and then

knock a ball through the wicket that would change
to a tiny pig on the other side, and when it got up to
run away—"

"Merlini?" Joel interrupted softly. "Merlini, can I
ask you something?"

"Why, of course, my boy. What is it?"

"Well—" Joel swallowed. "Well, I've just been
wondering about something. How do you make it
so that when I do your kind of magic, it works? Like

transformation. Is it the wand? Or do you do something yourself, besides?"

"Oh, you do everything, dear boy! That is—well, almost. I do command the *wand*," Merlini admitted.

"But sometimes, like when I'm weeding, you're not even around. I just find the wand in my pocket and it does what I want. And just now I practiced a whole string of transformations and you didn't even know what they were going to be—so how could you be telling the wand anything? I mean, you weren't even paying attention—you were talking."

"Yes, well, that doesn't matter. I just command the wand to do what you tell it to. And then it does, you see!" Merlini finished cheerfully.

"Oh," said Joel, feeling glad and sad and tremendously excited and tremendously upset and almost totally breathless, all at once. "I see. Can I try it again?"

"Certainly, my boy! Carry on. Now another little effect I'm considering for the ladies—perhaps the finale—is a peppermint candy tree. We'd start with the merest twig, I think, plant it in somebody's coffee cup, then make it grow and branch, and bear first mint leaves and then . . ."

By this time Joel had changed a stick to a petunia and an acorn to a chocolate bar, and made a large poison oak clump vanish. Then abruptly—because it was no use to shilly-shally—he turned to Merlini, touched him with the wand, and said, "Please go back where you came from."

It worked. Merlini was gone, in mid-sentence. So was the wand. So was the middle of Joel's stomach, at least it felt like it. He was quite alone in the woods, except for a tiny wisp of pink smoke just disappearing from the stump, a petunia growing oddly beside an oak tree, and a chocolate bar lying on the ground. Joel gazed earnestly at these items for a few minutes, blinking hard. Then he picked up the chocolate bar, which had a picture of stars and moons on its wrapper, and started home, feeling light-headed and light-footed, though not yet light-hearted. After a few steps he stopped, looked back at the stump, and said, "I'm sorry, Merlini. I did have to." A minute later, he added, "And *thanks*. Really. Thanks an *awful* lot."

Then he went on home, walking slowly and beginning to savor his freedom.

·11·

That evening, he ate the chocolate bar—but he never threw away the wrapper, in all his life. The next day, his mother helped him get out of his date at the Church Ladies' Fair. Within a week or so the whole wonder had died down, and Weirdo had work again, and people were talking of nothing but the Elm Hills Community basketball team, which had signed up a player eight feet tall.

As for Joel, he went back with relief to grubbing out weeds, playing baseball, and practicing sleight of hand, leaving evening stars severely alone. By the time he was twelve, he was pitcher, and getting to be a really good coin-and-card magician. One day his granny stopped by his door to watch him working on a new flourish—making a deck of cards fly in a rapid stream from one hand into the other. It was the first time he'd done it perfectly.

She smiled, and gave him an approving wink. "Practice does it, eh Joel?" she said.

"Yeah. Practice, practice, practice," Joel said with a grin.

But Sammy, who had wandered in to watch too, said, "I dunno. I kind of liked those real fancy tricks. Like the one with the canaries. Or the Saint Bernard. When are you gonna do that good Saint Bernard trick again, Joel?"

Joel smiled, and did the card flourish again, to make sure he had it right. "Oh—in about seven hundred years," he said.

ELOISE JARVIS MCGRAW—author, artist, and educator—is the creator of a dozen books for young readers. Mrs. McGraw's *A Really Weird Summer* won the 1978 Mystery Writers of America Award, and two earlier books, *Moccasin Trail* and *Golden Goblet,* were named Newbery Honor Books. She lives with her husband, writer William Corbin, in Lake Oswego, Oregon. They have a daughter and a son, and five grandchildren.

JIM ARNOSKY, a self-taught artist with a rapidly growing audience, has illustrated eleven books for children and written as well as illustrated six more, including *Nathaniel* and *Mud Time and More Nathaniel.* A regular contributor to *Cricket* magazine, Mr. Arnosky lives with his wife and their two children in South Ryegate, Vermont.